Reflections: Seasons 2015

An Anthology Celebrating the Seasons of the Year

Edited by Evelyn M. Zimmer

For permission requests, write to the publisher, "Attention: Permissions Coordinator", at the address below.
Zimbell House Publishing, LLC
PO Box 1172
Union Lake, Michigan 48387
www.ZimbellHousePublishing.com

© 2015 Zimbell House Publishing, LLC

Published by Zimbell House Publishing, LLC
www.ZimbellHousePublishing.com
All Rights Reserved

Print ISBN: 978-1-942818-04-5
Electronic ISBN: 978-1-942818-05-2
Library of Congress Control Number: 2015900453

Reflections: Seasons

2015

An Anthology Celebrating the Seasons of the Year

Edited by Evelyn M. Zimmer

Reflections: Seasons 2015 is a literary journal produced by Zimbell House Publishing showcasing the talents of new writers.

Within these pages are short stories and poems celebrating the seasons of the year. We hope you enjoy reading these new authors as much as we enjoyed bringing their new voices to you.

The works included in this anthology have not been edited, as these were contest submissions.

Acknowledgements

The production of this anthology could not be accomplished without the dedication and literary expertise of our Zimbell House team.

Our sincere thanks goes out to everyone who submitted for this anthology, for without you, there would be no new voices to tempt us.

The top three winning submissions are:

John Vicary for *On Europa*
~First Place Winner

Richard Koreen for *Oh Christmas Tree, Oh Christmas Tree*
~Second Place Winner

Jane Blanchard for *Squirrel*
~Third Place Winner

Contents

Autumn Leaves

By Sasha Kasoff

I am a leaf
That fell from the tree of misery
Or did I jump?
Wanting to float free
To at last settle
In an elsewhere
I have stared at
For so long

But once I let go
The wind picked me up
And carried me far away
Now my life is but a dream
Suspended on the breeze
I see many other trees
Rooted and stately
Knarled and strait
Each a community
Persecuting the one different leaf

Jump! I urge
As I tumble by
So they join me in the sky
Until all the air
Is a swirl of color

Until we are let down
And buried under
Cold white death
Steals our last breath
And so we leaves
Feed yet more trees

By Design

By Jane Blanchard

The patterns are spectacular:
Yellow loop de loops of pollen
On the square, red-clay tiles
That floor the screened porch,
Where the cat stays,
Each and every season,
Out of range of sprinklers,
Spared from leaves or straw,
Bedded beneath an old sweater
During the slightest chill,
But left for a spell each spring
In the care of a twice-a-day keeper,
While the home folk go
To a condo on the coast,
Near a sign that says,
"No pets allowed."
A mole, very much alive,
Blindly tries to find
A way back to dirt:
Round and around he goes—
Over and across he goes—
Anywhere and everywhere
To avoid another stint
In the teeth of the creature
That took him to this

Unearthly place to begin with.
In a corner the cat stretches—
Then slouches—then watches
What she set in motion
And doesn't want to end with—yet.
Ready to pounce,
She awaits the return
Of her people
To a welcome mat
Of her making—but not.

The Christmas Tree

By Jeremy Bush

The sharp edge of the axe head glows a faint silver, reflecting the moonlight. Spencer grips the wood handle tight in his right hand, his left hand holding onto his son's tiny fingers.

"Where are we goin', Daddy?"

"I'm taking you to where Grandpa used to take me. The same spot where we went every year, every winter, to chop down our Christmas tree. I wish there had been some snow for us—it's just always a little nicer to go chop down a Christmas tree in the snow." Spencer stops and sets the axe on the ground. He reaches inside his jacket and takes out a flashlight and twists the head until yellow light shoots out. Then he shines it on the ground and on the trees around them. "And it'd be a lot easier to see where we were going with all that white on the ground. Of course we could have come in the day, when it was light out. But Grandpa always brought me here at night. He always made sure it was a nice moonlit night like tonight is. It just wouldn't have been the same if I had brought you here when it was still light out. It wouldn't have seemed right."

Jason, Spencer's son, is beaming up at his father. "Okay, Daddy." He doesn't mind that it's at night and in the dark. To him, a six-year-old boy, it's simply an exciting, grand adventure.

"I can carry the axe for you, Daddy, if you need me to." He reaches down and grabs onto the very end of the handle and lifts it off the ground. This handle isn't meant for a small boy, and is so long that the axe head scrapes along the ground as Jason walks beside his father.

"Ah, here we go," Spencer shines the light on an opening in the trees. "There's the path right there. You see that stone," he points the flashlight on a bubble-shaped rock beside the entrance. "That's how we always knew it was the right path. I remember it now. I just haven't been here in a few years. The last time was before you were even born. It was...let me see...probably ten years ago. And that was the last time Grandpa came out here. Now it's too much of a hike for him. It wouldn't be so easy with his walker, you know."

Jason has been dragging the axe in his right hand, but he pauses a second and switches the handle over to his left—that way he can once more hold his father's hand. Spencer smiles down at his son, happy that Jason is still young. Young enough that he actually wants to help. And young enough that he thinks nothing of holding hands with his father. Spencer knows that soon—a year, maybe two—it will be this way no longer. Just when he's getting old enough to really be able to help (chores, yard work, anything) he won't want to. And there will be no holding his daddy's hand. And it will no longer be "daddy," but "dad."

But that doesn't matter right now...because right now Spencer knows that his son would do anything to help him. And right now his son is holding his hand and calling him daddy.

"You sure your hands aren't getting chilly at all, Jay?" Spencer asks, suddenly a little worried.

"No. It's not even really that cold, Daddy." Jason smiles—a certain type of smile that his father recognizes. A smile that says, "Oh, silly Daddy."

"Well, I got our gloves in my pocket if we need them, OK? Hey…I think, I think…yes, we're there."

Spencer and Jason are standing at the lip of a large bowl-shaped area, about six or seven acres in size. Pine trees cover the entire spot, starting with the rim of this bowl. As they stand looking at the trees, they can see the tops of the pines gradually curving—sinking lower and lower down—toward the bottom of this inverted dome. A light breeze is blowing, sending what appear to be waves of silver (the moonlight shining on the needles and branches) flowing up and down, and up and down the sides of the bowl. Jason has never seen anything like it before and to him it seems magical. Spencer hasn't seen it in ten years and to him also it seems quite magical. Neither says anything for a minute, captivated by the sheer beauty.

"I remember why Grandpa used to take me here every year," Spencer says in a whisper. "Let's start walking around and looking for a tree. You can pick out any tree, any one you want."

"*Any tree I want?*" Jason whispers back.

"Yup, any tree you want...just as long as it's not a hundred feet tall or anything," Spencer quickly adds, imagining his son finding the biggest, tallest, fullest tree he can.

"Do you think...do you think we can walk down to the very bottom?" Jason asks, still in a hushed voice.

And Spencer suddenly remembers how as a small boy, he always, every year, wanted to do the same. Every year he asked his father if they could go down to the center of the bowl. There was something about it that had seemed to draw him. All of the magic and mystery and beauty of the area seemed to trickle slowly down through each of the pine trees, flowing through each and every needle and branch and pinecone, converging at the very bottom. "Of course..."

Spencer and Jason walk hand in hand, as Spencer shines his flashlight on the path that is steadily leading them lower and lower down through the pines and closer and closer to the bottom of the basin.

Jason is silent for a minute, his mind thinking something over. Then he looks up at his father. "Daddy, whose land *is* this? Is this, is this *ours*?"

"Part of me wishes it was ours, it's so beautiful. But it's almost as good as if it was. This land belongs to the Murphys. Many, many years ago Grandpa did something to help them—what I don't know. Grandpa never has told me. Well, they didn't have a lot of money. But they did have just a little bit of land. And so they told him he could come that Christmas, and every Christmas they were alive and still owned the land, and get our family Christmas tree here. That was their way of thanking Grandpa. Even after Grandpa decided he couldn't come anymore they told me I still could. They've invited me every year—send me a card each winter to remind me. And this year I called 'em up and told 'em I'd be coming out one of these moonlit nights…and I'd be bringing my boy with me."

Jason is silent the rest of the walk down to the bottom, trying to guess what it was, what amazing thing Grandpa had done all those years ago to be thanked in such a glorious way.

As they get to the bottom, the very center of the bowl, Jason lets out a little gasp. There it is! The perfect tree.

"This one, Daddy! It's wonderful!"

Spencer can't help smiling to himself. It looks exactly like a few of the trees he can remember picking out as a small boy. Instead of the typical cone shape it has more of a round ball appearance—closer to a shrub than a tree. And he didn't need to worry about the height and whether it would fit in the car or the house, for this is one of the shortest trees in the woods—barely taller than Jason—only just over his head. Why it is his son would pick this tree over all others and why as a child he himself would also have picked this same tree, is a mystery to Spencer. But he is happy that his son is so excited about it.

"So this is the one, Jay?"

Jason holds the axe up for his father to take. "Yes! Just look at it. It'll be *perfect*."

Spencer takes the axe and lays it on the ground, resting it on the pine needles by the tree. "Here Jay, hold the light for me." Spencer puts the flashlight in his son's hands and then positions them so that the light shines at the base of the trunk. "Just hold it on that spot."

Then he picks the axe up and steps to the side of the tree. He spreads his legs wide and raises the axe over his head. The razor-sharp head slices deep into the bark. Spencer pulls the axe free and raises it up over his head again.

The axe slowly eats away at the trunk, forming a deep notch in the wood. Spencer stops to rest a minute and catch his breath. "I thought of bringing the chainsaw...but Grandpa always used an axe when he brought me here."

Spencer lets the axe head drop on the ground and leans the handle up against the pine tree. Then he takes the flashlight from Jason and using his fingers, rakes up a small pile of pine needles. He props the flashlight on this mound so that it shines on the trunk, right at the base where he is chopping.

"Now it's your turn, Jay." Spencer puts his hand on his son's shoulder and walks him to the side of the tree.

"Now stand with your feet apart. That's right. Now grab onto the handle. Put one hand right behind the other. Like this. Good. And then we raise it up over our head," and Jason, with his father behind him also holding onto it, lifts the axe up in the air.

"And then you let the weight do most of the work." And Spencer guides the axe down into a light chop of the trunk.

"What you do is try and hit it at an angle. You see how it cut part of it? After we do that a couple times, then we can swing straight into it and cut off all those chips...that's right, just like that. You're a natural at this, Jay!"

This praise makes Jason so proud he can't stop smiling. After another five minutes of chopping Spencer stops and takes the axe back.

"We almost got it. Now would you pick the flashlight back up for me? And stand back by that tree over there. Then when this one falls it won't be anywhere near you."

Jason is still smiling, still proud of getting to use an axe and chop a tree, "Okay, Daddy."

Spencer lifts the axe over his head and begins striking the tree again. With a few more strong blows the first cracking sounds of the tree starting to fall are heard. It drops in slow motion, the silver branches streaking through the night air, and topples over onto the pine needle-strewn earth.

"Well Jay, now I'm gonna need you to take both the axe and the flashlight. And you'll also have to lead us up the path while I drag the tree."

"Don't worry, Daddy. I can do it." And Jason, in his excitement over all these marvelous grown-up things his father is letting him do today, immediately runs to grab the flashlight and then the axe. Then he begins walking up the path, stopping occasionally to turn and shine the light back down and make sure his father is making it alright. And all those sad, melancholy thoughts that had just begun to form in his head over having to leave such a magical, wonderful place are driven—for now—from his mind.

Corn Maze

By Sasha Kasoff

We walked through the corn
As the dusk faded
And the stars poked out
The moon a storybook crescent
We went in circles
Eating sunflower seeds
Looking up at the stalks
Tips swaying above our heads
Taller and taller
As you are shrinking
Eventually you grow tired
Of the endless twists and turns
Despairing in the dark
Stalking through the rows
Shoulders hulking
Long strides
Soul set in determination
You got us out
And danced for joy
Under the black October sky

Edited by Evelyn M. Zimmer

Dancing with Summer

By Lauren Zlabinger

Summertime, the slow graceful dance
on tip toes through June's midnight moon,
where mornings dew kissed leaves
sparkle in early sunrise glances

July's heat brings showers that cool
bodies displayed
basking in summertime's
sunlit glaze

waiting patiently for breezes
cooling nights as sundown approaches
where graceful skies embrace
whispering to the trees

it's summertime, let's dance...

Fall Floral

By Lauren Zlabinger

While I busy myself
my eyes keep time
with the changing floral
Burnt orange asters
mixed yellow mums
dancing delightfully
in the warmth of the sun
to sweet smells of
ripening apples still
hanging from the trees
As I cut the last rose bloom
I close my eyes and see
summer as she quickly passes
right behind me

Edited by Evelyn M. Zimmer

Fallen Fruits

By Laurel Zlabinger

Wild as the vintage crocus blooms
as silvery moss of tongues
mingle among the woody vines,
twisting braids of ivy climb
winding round the apple
and the sweet perfume of plum,
fallen with the fruit of time
each season as in past
reaping what is offered
as the season dies so fast...

Jive Dive

By Jane Blanchard

This place gets busy in July.
We stand inside, three of us, queued,
Watching, with waiters passing by.

Once seated, oh-so-hungry, dry,
We long to order drinks and food
But watch waiters (damn!) pass us by.

With menu too-well-viewed, we try
To flag down any dame or dude.
This place gets busy in July.

With order placed at last, we vie
To see who has the least bad mood
While waiting, watching passersby.

When served ('bout time!), we satisfy

Ourselves till all is sipped or chewed.

This place gets busy in July.

To get the bill run, paid, we sigh

And signal, nothing rude or crude.

This place gets busy in July.

Wait! Watch us pass on a goodbye.

Late Summer

By Lauren Zlabinger

As late summer closes her eyes
resting like a volcano
wheat fields sway
golden and drenched
from the heat of summer rays
maze rises high above my head
tassels floating midair
calling to the bees
while beards of silk
change color in a breeze

we walk through meadows
overgrown with wildflowers
and wheat grass
stepping slowly in the heat
finding shade
against the cooling bark
of a little nook
tucked under an age old oak tree
hiding from the heat
of a late summer sun...

Oh Christmas Tree,

Oh Christmas Tree...

By Richard Koreen

"But Mom ..."

"Now Norman, patience."

"But Mom ..."

"I know you're waiting. We're all waiting."

"But I'm waiting most."

"Look out the window, here he comes now."

My Dad! And on the top of our blue '53 Plymouth, the tree! This was the real beginning of

Christmas. First the tree, then the decorating, then people coming to visit, then the food and the treats, and the picking out of stuff in the catalogue, and the...

Last year we had all gone out to the farm to get our tree. "The traditional way," as Dad said. We had gone with our skis and an axe and Dad lit a fire in the bush and we made tea and my feet got cold and...

"Put the skis on the roof rack. We can wear our ski boots."

"OK dear, I'll get the hot chocolate."

Dad put the three of us into the back seat and the rope and axe in the trunk. We were going to the farm. I couldn't wait to be at the farm in winter.

Jerry always stood on the hump in the middle, I sat behind Mom and behind Dad, Roger. He was twelve. I guess the oldest got to sit behind Dad. Jerry was so excited he was already bouncing.

"Stop that Jerry, You'll drive your Father crazy. Sit down. Sit still."

Jerry sat back and was still while Mom's eyes were on him. As her head turned to look at Dad, Jerry stood back up on the hump. We were off. The familiar ride through town settled us down but as we left the city streets our excitement rose. Soon we were turning off the highway onto the white and slippery side road, then the gate and the hill down to the barn.

Mom strapped my skis onto my boots. I didn't have real ski boots, just my usual winter boots. My bamboo poles were a bit too long for me. Mom said I would grow into them next year but she had said that last year and they were still too long. I didn't want to say anything, maybe I wasn't growing, maybe I would have to start eating all those things on my plate. Jerry had my two-years-ago poles. Mom said he would grow into them. His poles would have fit me better than the ones I had. If we traded only one of us would have too-long poles. Jerry could grow into them in four years. The thought made me laugh out loud as we plodded along.

Dad brought up the rear as we headed out behind the barn into the bush. No one lived at the farm anymore. I had never known of anyone living there but Mom and Dad kept talking about life at the farm. Mom made tracks for us to ski in and checked on our progress every second step. We were a slow parade.

Soon we were deep in the bush. This was my recollection but probably we were less than half a block into the trees. Dad picked a good spot. All the spots were the same but we had to look for a good spot.

"Right there, under that spruce," Dad said with authority, "We can build a fire and have some tea."

Fire soon blazed, but a bit too hot. The lowest branch burst into flame, released its load of snow and extinguished the fire in a hissing cloud of ash and smoke. We jumped back and Mom gave Dad that look. Dad was sheepish and tried to pretend he knew it would happen. None of us, well maybe Jerry, thought he had known but we let the presence stand.

Mom picked the location for the new fire. A stick was braced on a log to hang the water pot over the flames. Snow melted in the pot as we sat waiting for tea. We didn't usually get adult drinks and that made this a doubly special treat. Soon we had tea with milk and sugar and spruce twigs and a bit of ash. It was delicious.

My left heel got wet in the snow. I rolled over to show Mom my wet foot and yelled. I had twisted my right ankle. My right boot was still strapped to my ski. Jerry yelled and he threw his tea straight up behind him. It hit Dad in the seat of his ski pants. Roger laughed. I kept yelling in pain and Mom took two steps back. I think she was trying to understand what was happening. She stepped onto the knap sack and there was a sploosh sound. The lid had burst off the Tupperware jug drowning our lunch in hot chocolate.

Dad announced, "Roger, you'll have to carry Norman. He's not going to make it very far with a bad ankle. And it's not nice to laugh at your Mother."

"I wasn't laughing at…" Roger stopped mid-sentence, realizing he would be better off leaving Dad's re-construction of events. We made a very slow and cold retreat from our winter 'tea in the bush' adventure.

Dad angrily cut off the top of the spruce with the burned bottom branches and we had our Christmas tree.

It never did quite lose the smoky smell. I guess it was that smell that reminded us evening after evening as we told and re-told the ever more complicated story of the fire, the tea, the twisted ankle, the long walk back. Odd, no one ever mentioned Dad's wet pants. That year, the tree stayed up longer than ever, into late January. I hope it's a long Christmas this year too.

My mind snapped back to the present. Dad untied the tree from the top of the car and balanced it on his shoulder. He walked up the front walk, mounted the steps. The tree was obviously a heavy load for him but he managed. His coming through the front door looked funny. His head and shoulders disappeared into the body of the tree and it looked like the tree had legs. He popped out again as he rounded the corner into the living room.

Our house was small but comfortable. We had a few nice things from grandparents, such as the tri-light in the living room, the one with the swirling golden glass shade that stood in the bay window, a place of pride. But now that place would be for the tree. Mom had carefully pulled the tri-light off to the side. The other, older tri-light was across the room in its usual spot beside Dad's chair. Dad stepped out of his outdoor toe rubbers, walked into the room and turned towards the bay window. The tip of the tree snagged the old tri-light. CRASH!

All mouths gaped, eyes popped. Dad turned around, the tree swooped, CRASH! The swirling golden globe: a thousand pieces.

Dad calmly put the tree down, examined the golden shards, circled back to the old tri-light. There was one bulb left. He unscrewed it, raised it in the air and threw it crashing to the floor. He stomped out of the room.

Mom just managed, "Merry Christmas."

The Tri-light Christmas turned out all right. The lamp remains disappeared. No one mentioned anything about an accident, and we all decorated, cooked, and entertained. It wasn't as long as the Smoky Tree Christmas, but it wasn't a bad Christmas. The Tri-light Christmas has gone down in family history as one of the Christmas's that has its own name and gets talked about regularly.

On Europa

By John Vicary

In the seventy-five months since he'd touched down on Europa, Jenner had forgotten the taste of cheese. He'd forgotten other, lesser sensations, too, such as how the sun could burn his retinas during his morning commute if he wasn't careful to keep the visor down or the way water tasted on a summer day when he drank straight from the garden hose because he was too lazy to go into the kitchen. None of these problems existed on Europa, so he didn't think about what he was missing until one day more than six years into his stay he realized he couldn't remember cheddar anymore.

By rights, the wave of nostalgia should have hit him three months ago, on the anniversary of his landing, but that day passed shrouded in indifference with the brethren that bookended it. Instead, now, for no apparent reason, he found himself craving a hamburger with a thick slice of cheese, just like the one he'd consumed the day before lift-off. The memory was so sharp that his mouth watered and he could almost taste the tang of the cheddar mingling with the juice from that Blank Angus, hot from the grill. He wasn't one to reminisce, which made the stray longing that much harder to control. Jenner breathed through his nose until the wave of temptation passed, as it always did. It was just a matter of control and time. Jenner had time to spare.

They hadn't told him about the cravings during his training. They'd covered a lot of useful things he needed to know about living an isolated existence on a foreign planet—not a planet, he corrected himself. A moon. He sometimes fancied himself as the little prince, alone on his own world, but his de facto home was in reality only a satellite in thrall to the shadow of Jupiter.

Although he'd requested assignment on Titan, he could've done worse than where he'd ended up, Jenner surmised. The rest of the crew had envied him when the orders had come through. Jenner thought of poor Ramey's face when he found out he'd have to spend the better part of a generation locked up on Rhea. That's what it amounted to, after all. They were all like highly trained prisoners. They had all the room in the world, but where could they go? Who could they talk to? N.A.S.A. sure hadn't put that in the brochure when they'd asked for volunteers to go forth and test habitable climates.

That wasn't fair. Jenner shook his head. He had to get his mind right. Sometimes these moods came over him and he went a little crazy. The problem was that there was no one to bring him back to good sense. In the beginning, they'd had radio contact with astronauts on the nearest settlements. That's what N.A.S.A. wanted to call this solitary arrangement: a settlement. Jenner laughed to himself even though it wasn't funny. For a few years, he'd been able to talk to the guys who'd been stationed on Callisto and Ganymede, at least while their orbits were in sync.

The Saturnalian settlements could presumably keep in touch the same way, at least that had been the plan. Something had gone wrong about four years into the mission, and Jenner's comms had fried. He'd been operating on radio silence ever since. There was a procedure for that, and he knew how to carry on with the rest of his directives regarding testing of the pyllosilicates that comprised the surface matter, but it made for a lonely life. Jenner wondered if the other guys thought so, too, or if he was the only one cut off from the group. He wondered a lot of things that he'd probably never know the answers to.

The dreams had started not long after he'd arrived. Jenner had never been much of a dreamer; he'd always fallen into sleep as if it were a meal to consume with great relish. He'd wake, refreshed, ready to tackle his day without much thought to the time he'd spent in unconscious slumber. After Europa, however, he'd begun to lie awake before rest found him. He'd started to dream of events from his past, and when he woke he had difficulty parsing the truth from the fiction of his troubled mind. Had there been lavender bushes in front of his childhood home or had the stoop been clear of greenery altogether? Jenner didn't know anymore. He looked up into the sky to search for answers, but even the stars he'd always recognized seemed to mock him. Where was Orion and Gemini? Where were Ursa Minor and the Big Dipper? This new sky above him was wiped clean of any helpful punctuation in the darkness. He was an alien in a foreign country, and he felt the loss of home most keenly in dreams.

During the day, Jenner could shake his sentiment free. He had been given an important job to do, one that might take him twenty-five years or more to complete. His analysis of crust composites for viable organic material might be one of the most valuable tasks ever afforded an astronaut in the history of space exploration. On a lesser scale, he was here to study the theory of heat transfer from plate tectonics as well as he was able, and also to detect and scan the water vapor plumes that were unique to Europa and Enceladus. Jenner knew that he could work every day and he still wouldn't be able to furnish as complete a report as N.A.S.A. was expecting. He kept focused and he did his best. He had nothing to distract him from his work, after all.

There were times, though, when exhaustion dragged his bones to stop and his gaze flickered towards Titan. It had been within his grasp, and he still regretted that he hadn't been assigned there. That had been Lee's fate, and the officer had tried to keep the expression of desperation from his face when he'd found out it was his station, but he hadn't quite succeeded. The person going to Titan wasn't going to make history; it wasn't a viable environment, even by a long shot. Not for the next five billion years, at any rate. That was slated as a research mission. They'd all patted Lee on the back, sorry for him but secretly glad to have escaped with more promising fares. Jenner had made the appropriate noises of consolation, but he would have exchanged places if he could.

Titan was close to a dead moon, but it had weather. It rained liquid methane, and there were polar clouds. During a flyby, Voyager 1 had detected clear evidence of seasons. There was a winter, followed by a prolonged spring. Saturn shielded Titan from the solar wind, allowing for an atmosphere that included summer, during which it rained organic compounds. Lee was going to experience change. He was going to live on a moon that behaved, in some aspects, like Earth. It would be a little like home.

Jenner didn't realize how much he would miss the seasons until all trace of them had been demolished. Time was suspended in a frozen capsule of days here, with nothing to mark one from another. There was no change on Europa. All he could look forward to was an electronic tick on the calendar that shifted lines from 11/11 to 11/12. One little green bar to light up, that was all a day meant now to Jenner. The Fourth of July, his birthday, his anniversary … it was all merely a shift in electricity. These dates used to be imbued with meaning. Jenner remembered a time when Christmas meant snow and pretty lights and packages. His birthday had been near the last day of school, and as a child he'd always thought of freedom! Of the warm, humid air of summer beginning, and of long lazy days, spent in a glut of glorious relaxation. Halloween had always been his son's favorite holiday, and when Jenner thought of it, he'd always smell the caramel of the apples his wife would dip. He would think of the approaching chill of winter: almost upon them but not quite catching them yet. Halloween was the great herald of the long time to hunker down in eiderdown quilts and crackling fires. For his son, it no doubt would elicit memories of candy and roughhousing with the neighborhood kids, but as for Jenner, he thought of wood smoke and the winter ahead.

The dates on the calendar had always been so much more, but without memory and season to give them meaning, Jenner was left adrift in a void. What was 10/31except a set of numbers in a sequence that came before 11/1? What was 12/25 except the day before 12/26? What were any of them, really, when the years stretched out into infinity without change to mark them different in any way?

Jenner laid down to rest. He closed his eyes and dreamed of a drift of snow that had fallen when he was a child. He could still remember making a snow angel. He'd flapped his arms and legs over and over, wanting it to be perfect. It had to be just right. The cold seeped through his suit, but still he moved his arms. "Look," he told his brother. "I can fly! Someday I'm going to fly away from here, all the way into the sky."

When he woke up he couldn't remember the feel of snow. He couldn't remember his brother's face or what the blue sky looked like. He gazed up to see, but there was no answer in the perpetual darkness above him. All Jenner knew was that it was cold, and there was enough work to be done to fill a lifetime. He climbed to his feet and left dreams of angels behind.

Radio City Music Hall

By A.J. Huffman

Christmas in New York, and the lights are even
more garish than usual, strung in the shape
of a tree, twinkling above the crowds, filing in
to fill seats they are too excited to sit in. House
lights blink, announcing the show is about to begin.
The best legs in town kick their way onto the stage
to an eruption of applause, whistles, catcalls.
The Rockettes have arrived in reindeer and Santa
costumes, appropriately furred for the season.
The audience is transfixed, captured by the music
and glitter. For a moment the real world falls away,
and they too are flying among the stars
on magical cables, they believe are wings.

Edited by Evelyn M. Zimmer

September

By Evelyn M. Zimmer

Evalinne is restless. Ceafo has left the days correspondence on the tray by her bedside table, knowing full well her mistress was not going to sleep well with him away. Eva tosses off the thin summer weight sheet and drags herself out of the miserably empty bed. His shirt falls to her knees, tangling itself up in her thighs as she moves from the bed... absentmindedly picking up the letters as she passes.

Moving to the tall open doors of the balcony, she rests her head on the frame. *The goddess is restless tonight,* she muses as the clouds scurry past the quarter moon as if not wanting to block the startlingly bright light. Forcing herself not to dwell on the day's events at court she continues her short journey to the overstuffed chair that sits out there... *His chair.* Curling her legs underneath her, she sighs and gazes out over the landscape...the city is quiet tonight.

Returning her attentions to the letters in her hand, she flips through them distractedly...searching for the penmanship that will allow her some sign that he is still safe...finding what she longed for, she sets the rest underneath her leg to keep them from flying away...the breeze sultry at best.

"Eva-" she reads. No dearest...no endearment of any kind...this will not be the love letter she hoped for, when his letters begin so bluntly she knows it will be full of politics, daily events and the business of their lives. But still, she reads on knowing that their correspondences often mimic the conversations they have. This one is no different, full of his musing about the events he witnesses, the encounters he has, the randomness of thoughts...sighing as she finishes the letter, she lets her head fall back against the chair, scootching herself to a more comfortable position, the wind whips about her hair, the cloth of his shirt being pulled open, nearly exposing her full breast to the moon. She is restless.

With no interest in anything but keeping a semblance of contact with him she wanders into Ceafo's little office and lights a candle on the desk. Placing the remaining unopened correspondence on top of the neat pile of accounts Ceafo left open, she rummages for stationary, ink and pen. Morning is approaching quickly. Suddenly too tired to write him after all, she abandons her efforts and crawls back to bed...their empty bed.

The wind is hot. The air is caressing. The drapes are open and billowing with this...this...heat. Dawn is approaching...she tosses unable to sleep. Her blood is restless.

She listens to the dwindling night sounds and rolls over in the large empty bed, throwing off the sheet again. Her mind will not settle, time passes and then she hears the footman come up from the kitchens with the breakfast trays. She hears Ceafo complaining to the pretty little maid about making the water for her bath cooler today. Evalinne chuckles to herself thinking that Ceafo is always so concerned for her comfort. *Perhaps a nice gift is in order...*

Resigning herself to actually getting up and staying up, she returns for the discarded stationary, pen and ink, it is time to write him back.

My Love-

You know I love your rambles...the non-secateurs make me laugh...I can still hear your voice as I read your words...it's seven in the morning here...the hot lusty winds have been blowing all night....the wind chimes are frantic...the sun is shinning in its early morning golden glory...everything is aglow...I often times forget the beauty of the early morning hours...being of a vampiric nature...I rarely see them anymore...*chuckles*

The winds remind me of what I've heard called the madness winds of the Barrens...having never been, I can only assume...it's hot for late September...I saw my first turning leaves earlier this week in the forest, oh how I love the fall...then these strange winds came fast and hot late yesterday evening... with all windows open....my skin was caressed into remembrances of heated moments past...causing a slow burning lust to rumble about beneath the surface of my awareness...the sound of the wind in the pines-furious...searching...the breeze coming in through the windows causing the curtains to billow...it's almost sensual...watching them is almost erotic...the dance of the cloth against the moving air...

I'm afraid it is too sultry for sleep...the air is caressing me into a kind of madness...a desire driven thirst is humming beneath my flesh...It makes me think

of you...my wicked Master...this wind you sent to me
to keep me company until your return...

-Æ

She folds the missive, watching the wax heat...then drip...feeling the weight of her family signet, she seals the words that so inadequately describe her awareness of his torture. The winds kiss and caresses her flesh as she sits back in the chair, tossing the signet carelessly unto the desktop.

"It's going to be one of those days..." she mumbles to herself.

Squirrel

By Jane Blanchard

Here's a nut, and there's another,
On the ground's deep leafy cover.
Now is not the time for crunching
What will keep for future munching.
Pausing just to catch a breath
Might result in early death.
Not to worry, hurry, scurry;
Carry quickly, bury thickly.
Dash to stash an ample cache;
Don't be left with teeth to gnash.
Why be picky? Take them all;
Sort them later after fall.
Quibble less on autumn days;
Nibble more when winter stays.

What is fall?

By Lauren Zlabinger

It's saying goodbye
to sunlit days
where skin is tinged golden
in pools by the rays,

It's ending of slow walks
to a sun setting waltz
or sitting by the bay
when a breeze comes across,

It's the rustling of trees
laying waste of her leaves
some protection from the snow
all nature's comes to know,

Its chilled morning air
crisp cool nights
apple picking
pumpkins and spice,

Its shorter days
and longer nights
preparing ourselves
as winter strikes...

About

The

Authors

Jane Blanchard

Jane Blanchard studied English at Wake Forest before earning a doctorate from Rutgers. She currently divides her time between Augusta and Saint Simon's Island, Georgia. Her work has recently appeared in Concho River Review, Mezzo Cammin, and Orbis.

Edited by Evelyn M. Zimmer Reflections: Seasons 2015

Jeremy Bush

Jeremy Bush lives in western New York with his beautiful wife, Bekah, and their 3 year old son, Andy. Some of his publications include the Pulp Empire anthology *Pirates and Swashbucklers* and the Post Mortem Press anthology *Mon Coeur Mort*.

Edited by Evelyn M. Zimmer

A.J. Huffman

A.J. Huffman has published nine solo chapbooks and one joint chapbook through various small presses. She also has two new full-length poetry collections forthcoming, *Another Blood Jet* by Eldritch Press and *A Few Bullets Short of Home* by mgv2>publishing. She is a Pushcart Prize nominee, and her poetry, fiction, and haiku have appeared in hundreds of national and international journals, including *Labletter, The James Dickey Review, Bone Orchard, EgoPhobia, Kritya, and Offerta Speciale*, in which her work appeared in both English and Italian translation.

Edited by Evelyn M. Zimmer

Sasha Kasoff

Sasha Kasoff is a published poet, fantasy writer, and aspiring teacher. She has been writing poetry for over ten years and has wanted to be a teacher her whole life. Having recently returned from studying abroad in Ireland, she is currently attending University of the Pacific. Her poetry can be found in two self-published books of poetry as well as in anthologies, magazines, and other literary presses.

Richard Koreen

Richard Koreen is a retired teacher living with his wife Diane on the shores of Lake Winnipeg. His short stories are usually about personal experiences filtered through his very unserious, often madcap perspective. He's enjoyed writing since childhood and now finally has some time to spend attempting to entertain. He hopes you enjoy. For him retirement is a process of continually re-inventing himself. Who knows who he'll be next year.

John Vicary

John Vicary began publishing poetry in the fifth grade and has been writing ever since. A contributor to many compendiums, his most recent credentials include short fiction in the collections *Midnight Circus, We Were Heroes* and *Temporary Skeletons*. John is the Submissions Editor at Bedlam Publishing. He enjoys playing piano and lives in rural Michigan with his family.

Evelyn M. Zimmer

Evelyn Zimmer began her writing career in the second half of her life. While she has always had a love affair with the written word, it wasn't until now that she has had the time to dedicate herself to her passion. In her spare time she enjoys various activities with her friends and visiting her family across the States. She lives in her family home in Michigan with her husband Paul and the newest addition to their family, a Shih-Tzu named Leo.

Edited by Evelyn M. Zimmer

Lauren Zlabinger

Lauren Zlabinger is a freelance writer and poet. She writes and posts daily on her personal blog and she is an on- line editor for Exhaling Catalysts, both which are a part of the world wide artistic community of Tumblr. She currently resides with her husband in Tinley Park, Illinois where she works as care giver. Her projects include an anthology of life, love and loss, and she is currently writing an erotic romance novel, containing sex, intrigue, humor and a splash of danger. Her work has been published in *The MOON.*

Edited by Evelyn M. Zimmer